BAMBOOZLED

For my best friend,
and mentor, wife, Rhonda D.L.

ISBN 0-590-47990-3

14 13 12 11 10 9 8 7   4 5 6 / 0

Printed in the U.S.A.   08

The illustrations in this book were painted in watercolors.

BAMBOOZLED

DAVID LEGGE

SCHOLASTIC INC.

New York Toronto London Auckland Sydney

I love my grandpa.
I visit him every week.
And every week, things are
the same.
But *last* week when I arrived,
something seemed odd.

We sat down, as usual, and talked for a while. Then Grandpa poured two cups of tea, and we ate fresh pastries he'd bought that morning.

We played cards.

As always, he won.

We looked at his old
photo albums, and I listened
to his stories about
the good old days.

I helped him with the
housework, but something
still bothered me.

We worked in the garden, and I planted bulbs in the flower bed.

I pushed the wheelbarrow while Grandpa pruned the roses.
But still, something seemed odd.
It was on the tip of my tongue . . . .

"You *are* quiet today," Grandpa said as he fed the cat.

"I know," I said.
"I can't figure it out.
There's something I can't put
my finger on. Something,
today, seems odd."

"Well — I've redecorated the hallway."

No, it wasn't that.

"I've bought two new fish."

No, it wasn't that either.

Then, just as we were saying
good-bye on the doorstep,
it suddenly hit me.

"Grandpa!" I said. "That's what it is.

Your socks are odd — they don't match!"

Silly Grandpa.

We laughed and laughed!